This book belongs to:

_____

Dancing with the Wind

written by STANTON ORSER   illustrated by JAMES BERNARDIN

rising moon

Books for Young Readers from Northland Publishing

Always . . . —s. o.

To Emily and Anna Quayle, creative friends. —j. b.

The illustrations were rendered in acrylic
and colored pencil on coquille board
The text type was set in Esprit
Calligraphy by Judythe Sieck
Composed in the United States of America
Art Directed by Rudy J. Ramos
Designed by Mary C. Wages
Edited by Tom Carpenter
Production Supervised by Lisa Brownfield

Manufactured in Hong Kong by Global Interprint

FIRST IMPRESSION
ISBN 0-87358-639-5

Library of Congress Catalog Card Number 96-38111
Cataloging-in-Publication Data

Orser, Stanton, 1958-
Dancing with the wind / by Stanton Orser ; illustrated by James Bernardin.
p.   cm.
"A Justin company."
Summary: The animals of the forest conspire to rescue the wind from
a hunter who has captured her and locked her in a box.
ISBN 0-87358-639-5
[1. Winds—Fiction. 2. Animals—Fiction.] I. Bernardin, James, ill. II. Title.
PZ7.07465Dan   1997
[E]—dc20   96-38111

0584/7.5M/4-97

A note on the wind

The wind is important to every living thing. Winds are caused by the unequal heating of the earth's surface by the sun. Warmer air expands, becomes lighter, and rises. Cooler air rushes in from surrounding areas to fill the empty space. This process continues, creating a steady flow of air and bringing constant changes in the weather.

The wind plays a vital role in the community of plants and animals we call the ecosystem. In *Dancing with the Wind,* the wind and the creatures who band together to save her are all part of an interconnected ecosystem.

Tonight the wind is blowing hard against my house. I lie in bed listening to the walls creak and the windows shake.

"I'm afraid," I call to my father.

He picks me up and holds me in his arms.

"The wind is dancing tonight," he says. "Sometimes she dances with great power. She shakes trees and houses and anything in her way. Come look."

He carries me to the window, and we watch tree branches jumping back and forth and leaves racing across our yard.

"Did you know," he asks, "that long ago you could see the wind?"

I shake my head and snuggle against him as he settles into a chair and begins.

She was a beautiful woman with long, gentle breezes for fingers and hair. She would laugh and dance through the forest, pushing trees this way and that. She herded the clouds like sheep, and she brought the rains that let everything grow.

The animals all knew her, because she teased them. She rustled the leaves, and the mouse jumped, thinking she was the owl who wanted him for lunch. She waved the grass, and the rabbit darted into his thicket, afraid that she was the fox. She snapped a dead branch, and the deer bounded into the shadows, fearing she was the bear who could crush him with a single blow. She pushed down a tree, and they all jumped, thinking she was the hunter with his traps and dogs.

She would laugh and then sweep down and hug them, running her breezes through their fur.

The hunter knew the wind, too. He watched her dance from afar. She was so beautiful and powerful that he wanted her for his own. So he set out to catch her, and one morning he found her in one of his traps.

"I love you," he said, "and now you are mine." He sewed together a bag of skins and closed her in it. Then he stuffed the bag inside a large wooden box and locked it.

Without the wind's cool breezes, the air in the forest became stale and heavy. Trees dropped their needles and leaves. There was no more cover in which to hide. Without her rain the ground became hard and parched, and the grass died away. The rivers and streams dried up, leaving hard, muddy tracks. The only water left was a single spring. Unable to hide and hunt, the animals grew hungry. The bear thought, "I will wait until the deer goes to drink at the spring, then I will catch him."

The fox thought, "I will wait until the rabbit goes to drink at the spring, then I will catch him."

The owl thought, "I will wait until the mouse goes to drink at the spring, then I will catch him."

They all arrived together.

"FOOLS!" cried an old porcupine sitting on a nearby stump. The animals stopped and looked at her. They were all afraid of each other, but the porcupine jumped down from her perch and waddled among them, her quills glistening in the sun.

"All you can think of is your own bellies!" she said. "And yet have any of you tried to free the wind? Only she can bring us water and restore the forest. Without her we will all starve. Who among us has the strength and cunning to free her?"

"Not me," said the bear. "I have the strength to tear open the bag if I could get it in my paws, but I can't outrun the hunter and his dogs."

"Not me," said the deer. "I could outrun them, but I could never get close enough to snatch up the bag."

"Not me," said the owl. "I could fly in through a window and snatch up the bag, but the hunter keeps the wind in a box hidden in his cabin. I would not know where to find her."

"Not me," said the mouse. "I could find where she is hidden, but I could not unlock the box."

A small tick lifted his head from the neck of the deer.

"I could unlock the box," said the tick. "With my tiny legs and body, I could crawl into the keyhole and act as the key. But how will I reach the box? It is too great a journey for someone so small as me."

"And what of his dogs?" said the rabbit. "Who could creep close enough to unlock the box without being seen by them? If I stepped into the clearing around his cabin, they would run me down in seconds."

"I have tangled with his dogs," said the porcupine, raising the quills along her back and tail. "With these quills it is a fair fight." She thought a moment, then said, "Perhaps together we can help the wind."

That night the hunter's dogs lay lazily outside the cabin. They had not been out hunting since he brought home the wind. Suddenly the rabbit darted into the clearing and raced past their noses. They leaped up and gave chase, barking and yelping and nipping at his feet. The rabbit led them away from the cabin and into the woods where the old porcupine waited, and then he escaped into a thicket.

The dogs turned on the porcupine. They circled and nipped at her, but as they came close each caught quills in his nose and mouth. They growled and cried and sneezed and tried to turn her on her back, but the porcupine held them at bay, raising her quills like armor and swinging her tail this way and that.

While the porcupine battled the dogs, the fox slipped across the clearing to the corner of the cabin and set down the mouse, whom he had been carrying with his teeth. The mouse crept between two boards and into the cabin. He scampered from room to room, along the base of walls, under doors, and through crevices until he found the box.

"Here it is," he said to the tick, who was nestled deep in his fur. The tick clambered up the box and slipped into the lock. In a moment the lock clicked, and the tick poked his head out. "Open," he said.

The mouse scrambled to an open window. The owl circling above the house saw him and swooped silently into the room. He toppled the box, and it banged open on the floor. The bag rolled out, and the owl struggled into the air with it clutched in his talons.

The commotion woke the hunter, who lunged to the window in time to see the owl drop the bag in the clearing. He saw the fox drag it toward the trees, and then he saw the deer step into the clearing, hoist the bag onto his rack, and race off through the woods. The hunter called to his dogs, and they left the porcupine to chase after the deer.

Racing from the baying hounds, the deer bounded through the woods, leaping dried creek beds and fallen trees until he reached the spring.

There the bear, who had been waiting, rushed to him and grabbed the bag from his antlers. With a mighty roar, he set his claws into the skin bag and ripped it open.

The wind rushed out, blowing cool and clear, and bringing with her a steady torrent of rain. She raced through the forest dancing this way and that with fury and abandon. In her wake sprang up grass on the ground and leaves on the trees, and into this the animals all took cover from the hunter and his dogs.

Then the wind danced down the trail to the hunter and blew him into a creek. When he tried to get out, she blew him back in, so he sat in the shallow water and shivered.

"With my strength I could blow the life out of you," she said. The hunter cowered in fear, and the wind laughed at him. "You are a sorry animal," she said. "Never again will you know where and when I will dance. You will feel only the tease of my gusts and breezes to remind you of what you once knew." Still laughing, she vanished into the trees, and never again have people been able to see her.

Snuggled against my father, I wait as he pauses. He looks out my window, listening.

"She is in our yard now," he says. "You can't see her, but you can hear her laughing and dancing. She won't hurt you. She just wants to tease you with her power. Soon she will move on to somewhere else." He sets me back in bed, tucks in my covers, and kisses my forehead.

After he leaves I lie listening to the wind circling our house. I'm not scared anymore. I want to meet her and hear her laugh and see her dance.

Tomorrow morning when I go outside to play and a gust of wind blows my hair back from my face, I will hold out my arms, face into the breeze, and dance with her across our lawn.

About the Author and Illustrator

STANTON ORSER grew up as the oldest of five brothers and an extended clan of cousins who vacationed together each summer in Colorado. Sometimes in the evening, Stan and the other children would gather around the fireplace and he would tell them stories. *Dancing with the Wind* has its roots in one of those evenings. Twenty years later, the story has come to life in his first book. He lives in Beverly Hills, Michigan, with his wife, Therese, and their children, Renee and Nicholas.

JAMES BERNARDIN is a Seattle artist. When he's not illustrating children's books, he loves to go out to the Washington coast and feel the wind's mighty presence as it alters and shapes the landscape. He found it challenging and fun trying to express such a force in *Dancing with the Wind*. He is the illustrator of Northland's *Grandmother Spider Brings the Sun*. Jim lives in Edmonton, Washington, with his wife, Lisa, and cat, Emily.